JIGSAW LADY

Badger Publishing Limited, Oldmedow Road, Hardwick Industrial Estate, King's Lynn PE30 4JJ
Telephone: 01438 791037

www.badgerlearning.co.uk

JIGSAW LADY

TONY LEE

Jigsaw Lady ISBN 978-1-78147-811-0

Text © Tony Lee 2014
Complete work © Badger Publishing Limited 2014

Publisher: Susan Ross
Senior Editor: Danny Pearson
Publishing Assistant: Claire Morgan
Copyeditor: Cheryl Lanyon
Designer: Bigtop Design Ltd

2 4 6 8 10 9 7 5 3 1

CHAPTER 1

From the moment that Rickey Randall arrived at the school he had 'bully' stamped all over his face.

He was a good foot in height taller than everyone else in year nine, and everyone in class had heard a story from a friend, who had heard it from their brother, who had been told it in a bowling alley, about why Rickey had been expelled from his previous schools. Some said it was gang related. Some said he had almost killed a year seven while ramming his head down a toilet, but all said the same thing: Rickey Randall was bad news.

And for Billy Pearce and the other students like him, Rickey Randall was the Devil who had come to Ramsay High.

Billy was a small boy. He didn't really like his lessons, but he knew that if he wanted to be a postman like his father he had to learn his words and pass his tests. And he'd tried to keep out of trouble, making friends with the quieter boys in the class, Graham King and Martin Reilly. They'd spend their break times by the music block, playing handball against the sports' hall wall.

Unfortunately, it wasn't long until Rickey and his follower Dave Chapman found them. And, once he did, he decided to make their lives hell.

At first it was small things. During PE, Rickey would line the 'weedy' boys against the wall, using a tennis racquet to hammer balls at them. If they were hit they were allowed to leave. But Rickey would deliberately miss, building up the fear in the same way that a horror movie does.

The longer Billy stood there waiting to be hit, the more scared of being hit he became. It was torture.

From that, Rickey moved up to bigger games. When changing after PE he would steal Billy's clothes while Billy was in the shower and throw them in with him, soaking them. Or, worse, he would hide them so Billy had to run around naked looking for them. Usually he'd give them to the girls next door.

But the day that Rickey Randall pushed Billy out of the first floor window during French, holding him by his feet as Billy dangled in fear, was the day that Billy realised that he had to do something about this. The teachers didn't care, they were as scared of Rickey as he was and they were powerless to do anything. The only way that Billy was going to survive until year ten was to become a follower, like Dave Chapman.

Graham, however, didn't understand.

"You're joining the enemy!" he complained during Physics.

"No, I'm surviving," Billy said. "What would have happened in French if my shoe had slipped off? I'd have fallen! It wouldn't have been like a tennis ball hitting me! It would have been a dozen times worse! I might have broken something, even died!"

"I'd rather die than suck up to Rickey the Thicky," Graham muttered.

"I'm sorry," Billy said, "but I have to do something."

"If you do this, then our friendship is over." Graham sat back, folding his arms, and for a single moment Billy felt anger at his best friend.

"You're just worried that if I join Rickey, then I won't be the top of his hit list!" he snapped. "You're just worried that you'll be next! Some friend you are! Maybe we shouldn't be friends!"

And with that, Billy turned and stormed back to his desk, glaring at his one-time friend for the remainder of the lesson. But, deep down, Billy knew that Graham was right. If it had been the other way round, Billy would have said the same thing.

But he'd burned his bridges now and the only way to go was forwards. Straight towards Rickey Randall.

*

It was after Maths that Billy found Rickey and Dave behind the school canteen, slouching moodily against the wall, hands in pockets. Nervously, he walked over to them, expecting Rickey to leap up and attack him. Instead, Rickey just looked at him, his face becoming a sneer.

"What do you want?" he asked.

"I… I want to be part of your gang," Billy stammered nervously. Rickey looked over to Dave, who smiled.

"Why?" Rickey asked. Billy fought back the urge to reply *because that way you won't beat me up or throw tennis balls at me or strip me naked and make me run around…*

"Because I want to be cool," he lied.

Rickey laughed, pushing away from the canteen wall and leering at Billy. As Billy flinched back, Rickey placed an arm around his shoulder.

"You wanna join us?" he said. "You gotta prove it. You need to leave your old friends behind. You do that – you're in."

"I can do that," Billy said, already feeling guilty. Dave took a step towards Billy and gave him a hard stare.

"Let's see you do it then," he smiled. "Come on Rickey, let's go pay Billy's mates a visit."

Billy felt his stomach flip-flop as he followed the two bullies towards the music block. He wanted to turn around, to run away, but he found his feet following theirs, knowing that he was too scared to leave. As they turned into the small open area where Billy used to play handball, he saw with a sickening lurch of his guts that there was only one other student there.

Graham.

Standing still, a tennis ball in his hand, Graham had probably been playing handball alone, hitting the ball against the wall until someone turned up to play. Now he stood like a rabbit caught in the car headlights.

Rickey walked over to Graham, taking the tennis ball from his hand.

"Move," he ordered, pointing at the wall. Without even asking why, Graham quietly walked to the wall, facing the two bullies and Billy. Rickey gave Billy the ball.

"Throw it at him," he ordered.

Billy looked at Graham, seeing the hurt, anger and shame in his ex-friend's eyes.

"If you do, we're definitely no longer friends," Graham said softly. But Billy knew it was already too late. Shutting his eyes, Billy threw the ball, hearing the *ka-duk* of the ball missing Graham, hitting the wall and bouncing back. Picking it up, Rickey passed it back to Billy.

"Again," he said.

Three times Billy threw the ball; three times it missed, but the fourth time, the fourth terrible time, it flew straight at Graham's face, hitting his nose and drawing blood. As Graham ran off in tears, Rickey and Dave laughed, slapping Billy on the back. Billy felt sick. But at the same time, there was a small amount of hope that now he would no longer be bullied.

"Nice one," Rickey said. "You're almost there."

"Almost?" Billy looked from Rickey to Dave. "There's more?"

"Oh yes," Rickey grinned. "That was the proof. Now we need the initiation."

"What do you mean?" Billy wanted to leave. Dave leaned in close.

"We mean a test, something bigger than this. Tonight you join us on a mission," he said. "Tonight we meet the *Jigsaw Lady*."

Billy felt a shiver of fear run down his spine. He knew the stories about the Jigsaw Lady, and he wanted more than anything in the world never to visit her house. But he knew that whether he went that night would be based on who he feared more… the Jigsaw Lady… or Rickey Randall?

CHAPTER 2

The Jigsaw Lady wasn't some kind of horror story aimed at scaring children; she was a real person, one who lived in the broken-down old house at the top of Stone Hill. Ever since he'd been a small child, Billy had heard the stories about the Jigsaw Lady. Some said she was a lonely old woman who spent her days putting jigsaw puzzles together, but others said darker things: that she was a witch; that she'd been alive for hundreds of years; that she stayed young by drinking the blood of teenage boys; and how children, cats and dogs had mysteriously disappeared when walking through her gardens.

Billy didn't know which of the stories were true, but the one thing he did know was that the last thing he wanted to do was be anywhere near the Jigsaw Lady's house at eight o'clock at night. But here he was, at five minutes to eight, standing at the end of Stone Hill, waiting for Rickey and Dave to turn up.

It was another ten minutes before they arrived, and Billy thought he saw a slight trace of fear in their faces as they walked up to him.

"You made it then," Dave said as he stopped. Billy nodded.

"Why are we here?" he asked.

Rickey grinned, the fear disappearing from his face for the first time. "To have some fun," he said, opening the gate and entering the Jigsaw Lady's garden. "Come on."

Dave looked at Billy. Billy looked back at Dave.

Neither of them moved. Rickey, seeing this, sighed as he walked back out of the garden.

"And I thought I hung out with the hardest kids in school," he mocked. "But no! Here they stand, scared of a little old lady and some broken bits of pictures."

"It's not that," Dave said. "I've heard things, you know? Bad things. If she was to catch us in her garden…"

"Well she won't," Rickey said with a sneer on his face. "She's at Bingo tonight."

"What?" Billy stared at Rickey in shock. The thought of the Jigsaw Lady going to Bingo was one that had never occurred to him before. Did witches even play Bingo?

"Yeah," Rickey carried on. "My gran sees her there every week without fail. So she's not here tonight."

"So why are we here?" Billy asked. Rickey's smile faded away and Billy started to tremble as Rickey moved closer.

"Because we're gonna break in," he hissed. "We're gonna break in and bring all of her stupid jigsaws outside."

"Then what?" Billy couldn't stop himself from asking the question.

"Then? Then we're gonna empty them all on the grass and mix them up!" Rickey laughed. "Let's see her try to put them all back together after we do that!"

Rickey paused, looking at Billy.

"You do want to be in this gang, don't you?" he asked. "I mean, you don't want to be one of the bullied again, do you?"

"No, no," Billy shook his head, "not at all."

"Good," said Rickey. "Then let's go and have some fun."

They walked through the garden, Billy jumping at every noise he heard, convinced that at any moment the Jigsaw Lady was going to spring out of the shadows and turn them all into frogs – or worse. But nothing happened and, by the time they reached the Jigsaw Lady's front door, Billy was even starting to relax.

BAM! BAM!

Billy leaped into the air, only to see Rickey, his hand on the door knocker, laughing loudly.

"Did the nasty door knocker scare you?" he laughed. Billy sulked. As nobody answered the door, Rickey took a step back and, with a kick of his heavy black boot, he stamped at the door lock.

"What are you doing?" Billy asked, looking around in case anyone had heard them.

"How else are we getting in?" Dave asked, standing beside Rickey and joining in, his own boot slamming against the door lock at the same time as Rickey's. Under such force the door splintered open, swinging into the house.

"Bonus time," Rickey said as he entered the Jigsaw Lady's house. Billy didn't want to go in; he was too scared. Luckily he didn't have to, as a few seconds later Dave appeared with a handful of boxes in his arms. Each box was a jigsaw.

"Make yourself useful if you're not coming in," he said, throwing the boxes at Billy. "Make a pile of the bits in the middle of the garden, yeah?"

As ordered, Billy walked into the garden and started to open the boxes, pouring the jigsaw pieces onto the ground, throwing the boxes aside as he did so. Pictures of mountains, kittens and city streets all went flying as, box by box, the pile grew. Whenever Billy ran out, Dave always had another armful to add to the pile. Slowly, the pile grew higher and higher, now almost as tall as Billy was himself. He felt bad for doing this, for causing anyone, even if they were a witch, such hassle. But, at the same time, he wasn't being bullied and that counted for something.

Finally Rickey came out with the last three boxes, helping Billy and Dave throw the pieces onto the pile.

"That's it," he said. "Every jigsaw that the Jigsaw Lady owns."

"I don't want to be here when she tries to put them together," Billy said, staring at the pile. Rickey laughed as he reached into his pocket.

"Who said she was gonna get a chance to?" he said as he pulled out a tin of lighter fluid, squirting it all over the pile of jigsaw pieces as he danced around it. "I'm not letting her have any of these back. She's a witch. And you burn witches."

He paused, throwing the empty tin of lighter fluid to the grass as he pulled out a box of matches. Silently he removed one from the box and lit it.

"And if you don't burn the witch, you burn the next-best thing," he hissed, as he dropped the still-lit match onto the pile.

As the match hit the fluid, the pile of jigsaw pieces went up in flames, easily twice the height of the pile. Billy had to step back as the heat from the bonfire was so fierce.

"Come on, let's get out of here!" Dave pulled at Billy's arm. "Before someone calls the police!"

In a daze, Billy followed the two bullies out of the garden. But as he ran, he couldn't help himself. He stopped and turned, taking one last look past the bonfire, now blazing fiercely, at the Jigsaw Lady's house. And what he saw chilled him to the bone.

In the top right-hand corner of the house was a small, square window. And, as the light from the bonfire hit it, Billy could see a face staring out, a wrinkled old bag of skin that stared angrily down at the jigsaws, the fire, and at Billy. As their eyes locked, Billy realised exactly who he was looking at.

Rickey had lied. The Jigsaw Lady wasn't at Bingo. She'd been upstairs, asleep. And now she was staring at him. She'd seen what they'd done. She'd seen their faces.

And the Jigsaw Lady would want revenge.

Terrified, Billy ran from the garden at a sprint, hoping that if he could get away quickly he'd escape the Jigsaw Lady's curse. But at the same time he knew that if the Jigsaw Lady was a witch, and if she did curse them… then Rickey, Dave and Billy were dead!

CHAPTER 3

When Rickey dragged Billy into the boys' toilets, Billy thought for a moment he was back to the old days of beatings and being made to look stupid, but it was far worse.

For the three days that had followed the burning of the Jigsaw Lady's jigsaws, all three of them had been nervous, jumpy even. Nothing had happened on any of these days and Billy had even started to relax. But on the fourth day, as he was walking to Maths, Billy was grabbed by Rickey and pulled into the toilet, where he found Dave standing, his face pale and scared.

"What's going on?" Billy asked.

"Dave saw the Jigsaw Lady," Rickey said.
"He was in the supermarket and she appeared
out of nowhere. Pointed her finger at him and
cursed him."

Dave looked as if he was going to be sick.

"What happened then?" Billy asked. Dave looked
to Rickey, who nodded. Slowly, Dave removed
his tie and unbuttoned his shirt. Pulling it off his
right shoulder, he stared at Billy, tears in his eyes.

"This happened," he said.

There was a mark on Dave's shoulder. A
jigsaw-shaped mark. But when Billy looked
closer he saw that it wasn't a mark, oh no –
it was worse. It was nothing. A jigsaw-shaped
nothing that he could see the wall behind
Dave through. It was as if someone had taken
a photo of Dave and removed a part of it.

"I've got three of them," Dave moaned. "One on the shoulder, one on the hip and one… well, let's just say that going to the toilet might be a problem for a while."

"Four," Rickey said, pointing at Dave's right arm where a smaller hole in his body could be seen. "No, look. Five."

Dave started to cry, big shuddering sobs that scared Billy even more. For this bully to be so scared…

"So, what now?" Billy asked. Rickey shrugged.

"I dunno," he said, but stopped as the toilet door opened and Mike Wood from year eight walked in, staring at the half-naked Dave.

"What's going on?" Mike asked. Dave looked to Rickey. Rickey looked to Billy.

"Mike, can you see anything wrong with Dave's shoulder?" Billy asked. Stepping forwards, Mike stared right at the missing, jigsaw-shaped hole.

"Maybe a bruise coming up?" he said.

"You don't see anything… missing?"

"Should I?" Mike stepped back, looking at all three bullies. "I don't know what game you're playing but it's not good enough to get you out of school. Try harder." And with that, deciding that he didn't actually need the toilet, Mike left.

"He couldn't see it," Billy said. "Only we can."

"Maybe it's not real then?" Rickey said, looking to Dave. "Maybe it's like a big joke?"

"It don't feel like a big joke," Dave snapped back, pulling on his shirt. "It feels like I'm being torn apart, piece by piece."

"Look, let's give it a day and see what happens," Rickey said, and Billy knew that Rickey was scared, too scared to get involved. Dave shook his head.

"No, I'm not waiting," he pushed his school tie into his bag as he started for the door. "I'm going to her house and I'm gonna demand that she returns the bits of me she's stolen."

He looked at Billy.

"You coming with me?" he asked. Billy looked at his feet. The last place in the world he wanted to go was the Jigsaw Lady's house.

"You're both cowards," Dave hissed. "I thought I was hanging with the cool kids. Well, when I sort this out you can both go to hell. I don't want anything to do with you any more." And with that he stormed out of the room.

"Dave, wait!" Rickey shouted at the now closed door, but it was too late. Rickey looked back at Billy.

"We don't tell anyone," he hissed. "We keep this to ourselves, OK?"

For the first time, Billy agreed with him.

*

They didn't see Dave for the rest of that day, and nobody called during the evening. Billy spent most of the night in his room, standing in front of a full-length mirror, waiting for bits of his body to disappear. But nothing happened. And the following day he went into school wondering if Dave had lost any more pieces, or whether Rickey had been right and it was just some kind of sick joke.

The one thing he wasn't expecting was the policeman who appeared during assembly.

As soon as the policeman took the stage, Billy felt a cold hand of fear travel down his back. Was the policeman there because of what they'd done? Was he there to arrest them? He could see Rickey across the hall, looking over to him with the same expression on his face. Where was Dave?

"If anyone knows where David Chapman is, could they please contact us," the policeman said. "His parents are very worried."

"What happened to him?" Billy couldn't help himself as he blurted the question out.

"We don't know," the policeman replied. "All we know is that at nine o'clock last night we found a pile of his clothing on Stone Hill. What he's wearing, if indeed he is wearing any clothes right now, is unknown to us."

Billy kept his mouth shut after that, but he could see from Rickey's face that he had arrived at the same answer: Dave had run out of jigsaw pieces and had simply disappeared, either as he walked to, or away from, the Jigsaw Lady's house. He was gone.

Dead.

And as the classes walked out of the hall, Rickey made his way over.

"We need to talk," he hissed.

"About Dave?" Billy asked. Rickey shook his head.

"I don't care about Dave," he muttered. "He walked away from us, he insulted us. It's his fault he died. I wanted to talk about *this*."

He held up his hand and Billy saw that there was a jigsaw-shaped hole in it. Rickey was fading away, just like Dave had.

"I'm next," Rickey said, looking around. "I'm gonna die, just like Dave."

Billy shook his head.

"We'll work it out," he said. But secretly he knew that Rickey was right. If it was anything like what had happened to Dave, Rickey would be gone by tomorrow, nothing more than a pile of clothes on the floor. And Billy?

Billy would be next.

CHAPTER 4

Billy spent the rest of the day avoiding Rickey, too scared to see what other pieces of his one-time bully had now disappeared. But the final lesson was extra Maths, and Billy found himself sitting two rows behind Rickey, able to see the whiteboard through the large, jigsaw-shaped hole in Rickey's head. With one eye being almost all that was left, Rickey wasn't able to speak to Billy, he just kept looking around and staring, the one eye wide and filled with tears. Billy kept looking away, looking at anything but Rickey as, in front of his very eyes, he saw another jigsaw-shaped hole appear, removing Rickey's left ear.

Graham, sitting beside Billy, looked at him.

"Will you stop fidgeting?" he hissed. "I'm trying to listen to the teacher and you're distracting me." He looked over to what remained of Rickey.

"Why don't you sit with your new best friend?" he asked mockingly. Billy choked back a tear.

"Look at him!" he hissed back. "Don't you see anything wrong with him?"

"Are you OK?" Graham asked. "Are you on drugs? Did they get you doing bad stuff?"

"He's disappearing!" Billy hissed. "You can't see it, but I can! Why do you think he's so quiet! His mouth's gone!"

Graham stared at Billy for a moment.

"You really believe this, don't you?" he asked. Billy nodded.

"We were cursed by the Jigsaw Lady," he said. "We burned her jigsaws – well, Rickey burned them, we just emptied them outside. And then Dave disappeared, piece by piece. And now Rickey is, too."

"Wait, are you saying that Dave's clothes were found because he ran out of jigsaw pieces?" Graham started to chuckle. "That's just…"

He stopped as, in front of him, Rickey stood up and staggered towards Billy. All that was left of him that Billy could see was one eye and three fingers of his left hand. Billy started to scream as the horrible figure staggered towards him…

And then the last pieces disappeared. The now empty school uniform of Rickey Randall fell to the floor.

The class turned into chaos. The teacher was crying for calm, shouting that wherever Rickey had hidden, this wasn't funny and he should come out now, and the other students were cheering, saying it was the best trick they'd seen. But Billy looked at Graham. He might not have seen the pieces disappear, but he had seen Rickey fade away in front of his eyes.

"Now do you believe me?" he asked. Silently, Graham nodded.

"Will you help me?" Billy grabbed his one-time friend's arm. Graham snatched it back.

"You hit me with a tennis ball. You gave me a bleeding nose."

"I know, but I thought it was the only way to stop being bullied."

Graham stared at the pile of clothing on the floor. "And how's that working out for you?" he asked. He looked away for a moment.

"Look, I'll help you but only because we used to be best mates," he said. "And I'd hate to have to explain to your mum why you've disappeared. But you'll have to prove yourself again to me. We can't go back to what we were."

"I'll take anything," Billy said, smiling for the first time in four days. "So what do we do?"

"We go to the Jigsaw Lady," Graham said. "We go to her and beg for your life."

When Rickey Randall didn't appear after the lesson, school ended early and Graham and Billy went to Stone Hill to face the Jigsaw Lady. Walking through the garden, Billy saw with shame the burned patch on the grass where, less than a week ago, he had helped burn all of the Jigsaw Lady's puzzles.

Nervously, he knocked on the repaired front door. Three heavy hammers on the door knocker, and then a tense couple of minutes waiting for an answer. Nothing happened.

"She's not in," Billy whispered to Graham. "We should go."

"Wait!" Graham stepped back and looked up at the house.

"Hello!" he shouted to the windows. "My name is Graham and I wasn't part of this, but I really think you should listen to my friend here."

He paused. There was no sound.

"You're right," he said. "I don't think she's – "

He was stopped by the sound of the front door creaking open. Looking at each other, Billy and Graham pushed at it, opening the door wide.

There was nobody there.

Slowly, Graham entered the house, Billy walking in behind him. He hadn't been in the house last time, so Billy didn't know what to expect.

It was dark, with the curtains pulled against the light. There was a terrible smell coming from the kitchen and the sound of something bubbling on the stove could be heard. There was a window in the middle of the main room, a table beside it, and a chair backing against a large, open fire. A lamp and a bookcase were the only other things in there. The carpet was old and worn, the wallpaper was peeling. It looked like a house that hadn't been lived in for years.

An old woman appeared suddenly, standing at the door to the stairs. Billy jumped in shock, a little scream coming out of his lips as she walked into the room, staring at him. She wore a grey dress that looked as if it was once very colourful, but had never been washed. Her hair was wild and stringy and looked as if it hadn't seen a comb in years. Her face was wrinkled and one eye was closed as she stared at Billy in anger.

"You're one of them," she whispered. "You're one of them."

Billy nodded, too scared to do anything.

"I am, and I'm really sorry," he said, looking at Graham for support. "I didn't want to be bullied any more, and I thought that joining them would stop that. But I didn't know they were going to do this."

"And yet when you did find out, you did nothing."

Billy shook his head. "I was scared," he said. "I thought they'd just mix the puzzles up and run away. I was going to come back later and help you put them in the right boxes. I didn't know Rickey had the lighter fluid."

"You destroyed all of my jigsaws." The Jigsaw Lady walked over to the table, sitting down slowly in front of the fire. "But I'm making new ones."

Billy saw the two jigsaws on the Jigsaw Lady's table. They were small, each one a simple sketch of a boy in school uniform. It was a familiar uniform and, with a sick feeling in his stomach, Billy recognised both of the boys in the pictures.

Rickey and Dave were in the jigsaws,
frozen forever.

And they were screaming.

CHAPTER 5

"So tell me, what do you want, boy?"
The Jigsaw Lady smiled, a toothless grin that
did nothing to make Billy feel any safer. By the
light of the fire, the flames made the pictures of
Rickey and Dave look as if they were screaming
and moving around in pain. Graham nudged
him, waking him back up.

"I want… I don't want to be like them,"
Billy said, pointing at the jigsaws. The Jigsaw
Lady nodded.

"And what are you going to give me that will stop
me doing this to you?" she asked. Billy looked
around in terror.

"I don't know," he whispered.

"You're not the first to come here," the Jigsaw Lady said as she got up from her chair and walked into the kitchen, taking a large spoon and pouring some of the terrible smelling liquid into a cup. Walking back in, she offered it to Billy.

"Coffee?" she asked. Billy didn't know what it was, but the one thing he knew it wasn't was coffee. He shook his head.

"What do you mean, Billy's not the first?" Graham asked. The Jigsaw Lady made a strange coughing noise, a *hur-hur-hur* sound that Billy suddenly realised was laughter.

"The other two both came to me," she said as she sipped from the mug. "Each of them offered to do anything I wanted, blaming the others for the 'game' that they played on me." She stared hard at Billy.

"Would you call it a game?" she asked. Billy shook his head.

"No, I wouldn't either. And I let them tell me what they would do. And when I didn't like their answers, they shouted at me, tried to threaten me. Are you going to do that?"

Again, Billy shook his head.

"Then what are you going to do?" The Jigsaw Lady sat back down by the fire. Putting the mug down on the jigsaw of Rickey, the hot liquid splattered onto the picture, and Billy thought he could hear a faint scream of pain.

"Tick-tock," she said. "You don't have much time to decide."

Billy looked around the room, trying to think of something that he could do to make up for his crime. All he could think of, however was the fact that if he didn't think of something fast, he'd soon be a jigsaw like Rickey and Dave, the only two she now had, being taken apart and put together daily…

Suddenly Billy had an idea.

"We took your jigsaws from you," he said. "It's only fair that I get them back for you. I mean, I know I can't get you the same jigsaws, but I'll bring you a brand new one every week. And as I get more money, I'll bring you more. I'll hunt every charity shop, I'll go on eBay, I'll bring you as many jigsaws as you lost and more."

The Jigsaw Lady thought about this for a moment.

"And these two?" she asked, pointing down at the jigsaw pieces.

"When I've done what I said I would, you can decide what to do with them," Billy replied, secretly hoping that the Jigsaw Lady would keep them. As much as he felt bad about it, the idea of school without Rickey and Dave sounded far better than the idea of school with them back.

The Jigsaw Lady nodded.

"Fine," she said. "Bring me a jigsaw a week and we'll see how it goes."

Billy smiled in relief. "Thank you," he said as he started to back out of the room. "I'll bring you the first one tomorrow."

And with that, Graham and Billy left the Jigsaw Lady's house. Back in the sunlight of the garden, Graham looked at Billy.

"She didn't seem that bad," Graham said.

Billy didn't stop laughing all the way home.

*

Billy kept his word, and the next day he arrived at the house with a five-thousand-piece jigsaw of the Eiffel Tower in France. A week later it was a picture of William Shakespeare. He never entered the house again, he just placed the jigsaws on the ground, banged the door knocker and ran away.

The weeks turned into months. Billy and Graham became friends again, although never the best friends that they once had been. School ended and, after the holidays, Billy returned as a year ten.

At the same time, something odd happened to Billy. He started to grow, finally catching up with the other boys in his class. He also started to fill out a bit more. Graham even joked that Billy was starting to catch a few looks from the girls. After all, he was a local celebrity, the last boy to see Rickey and Dave alive. Again, the stories changed. Rickey and Dave were on the run from a drug gang, or the police, or they had been hired as secret agents... only Billy knew the truth, and he kept quiet.

And every week, without fail, Billy left a jigsaw on the step of the Jigsaw Lady's house.

But after a year had passed and nothing bad had happened, Billy started to get distracted, mainly by Jenny Davies, a new girl in his class. He'd asked her out to see a film and she'd said yes, but he'd realised at the last moment that by paying for the tickets he'd not kept enough aside for that week's jigsaw. And so he had gone to the Jigsaw Lady's house and left a note, explaining that he'd bring two the following week. And he kept that promise. But, knowing that he could miss a week meant that he started to miss several weeks, as other activities took up his time. After all, he'd given the Jigsaw Lady over sixty jigsaws by now, maybe even a hundred. He didn't remember burning that many. Maybe he'd fulfilled his debt and she simply hadn't told him?

And so, against Graham's advice, Billy left a note on the Jigsaw Lady's door, saying that he felt that he'd kept his side of the bargain and that she should enjoy the jigsaws that she had now as he wasn't bringing any more. And, feeling good about himself, he went to see a film with Jenny.

It was a few weeks later when the Jigsaw Lady came back into Billy's mind. It was almost summer break again, and Billy had decided that, as a gift, he'd find a few more jigsaws and pass them on to the Jigsaw Lady as a thank you. But, when he took his shirt off to get ready for gym, he saw Graham staring at him in horror.

"What's up?" he asked, knowing with a sinking, sickening feeling that he already knew.

"Your shoulder," Graham replied, pointing. "Look."

Billy went to the mirror and looked at his shoulder, knowing what he was going to see. It was small, almost too tiny to make out, but it was there. And as Billy stepped back, tears welling up in his eyes, he thought that he could hear laughing, the laughter of a mad old woman, from far away. Billy knew he was dead, doomed to be a sketch on a jigsaw, to live the rest of his days in a silent scream…

Because a small, jigsaw-shaped piece of Billy Pearce was now missing.

THE END